Pout-Pout Fish
Goes to the Doctor

Written by **Wes Adams**   Illustrated by **Isidre Monés**

Based on the *New York Times*–bestselling Pout-Pout Fish books
written by Deborah Diesen and illustrated by Dan Hanna

Farrar Straus Giroux
New York

With thanks to Dr. Patrick W. Kemper

Farrar Straus Giroux Books for Young Readers
An imprint of Macmillan Publishing Group, LLC
120 Broadway, New York, NY 10271

Color separations by Embassy Graphics
Printed in China by RR Donnelley Asia Printing Solutions Ltd., Dongguan City, Guangdong Province
Designed by Aram Kim
First edition, 2020
10 9 8 7 6 5 4 3 2 1

mackids.com

Library of Congress Control Number: 2019940837
ISBN: 978-0-374-31050-9

Our books may be purchased in bulk for promotional, educational, or business use.
Please contact your local bookseller or the Macmillan Corporate and Premium Sales Department at
(800) 221-7945 ext. 5442 or by email at MacmillanSpecialMarkets@macmillan.com.

Mr. Fish woke up feeling terrible. He didn't want to get out of bed.

His friend Mr. Eight came to visit. "What's the matter?" he asked. "Are you sick?"

"No," said Mr. Fish. "I'm worried about going to the doctor for my checkup today."

"Checkups help you stay healthy," Mr. Eight said. "A visit to the doctor is nothing to worry about."

"I know, but I can't help it," said the Pout-Pout Fish. "Will you come with me?"

"I'd be glad to!" said Mr. Eight.

On their way, they saw Miss Shimmer, who said doctor visits gave her the shivers.

"I don't like how cold the doctor's stethoscope feels on my scales," she explained.

"But that's how she checks how strong your heartbeat is," said Mr. Fish. "It's nothing to fret about."

"I guess you are right!" she said, and gave him a warm smile.

Ms. Clam and Mrs. Squid mentioned their own worries when they heard where their friend was going.

"I don't like when the doctor weighs me on the scale," said Ms. Clam. "It feels like I'm riding on a surfboard."

"But that's how she finds out how much you have grown," said Mr. Fish. "You shouldn't let that throw you off balance."

"I guess you're right," said Ms. Clam.

"I don't like the crinkle of the paper on the exam table," said Mrs. Squid.

"The doctor uses new paper under each patient to help keep the exam room clean," said Mr. Fish.

"Good point," she said. "Squids are squeamish about sharing germs."

In the waiting room at the doctor's office, Mr. Fish's pout got bigger and bigger.

"I don't understand," said Mr. Eight. "You've helped everyone else with their worries. What are you nervous about?"

Mr. Fish was quiet for a moment. Then he finally said what he was afraid of. "I don't like getting shots," he confessed. They made him think of sharp teeth and pointy spines.

"A shot is just a little pinch, and then it's over," said Mr. Eight.
"That's right," said the doctor as she ushered Mr. Fish into her exam room. "And the medicine in shots helps keep you from getting sick."

In the exam room, the doctor weighed Mr. Fish and measured him from tip to tail.

She used a light to look in his eyes and throat.

She took his temperature.

She listened to his heartbeat.

The doctor was gentle and kind . . . even when she gave the Pout-Pout Fish a shot.
"That wasn't bad at all!" said Mr. Fish. He asked for two bandages.

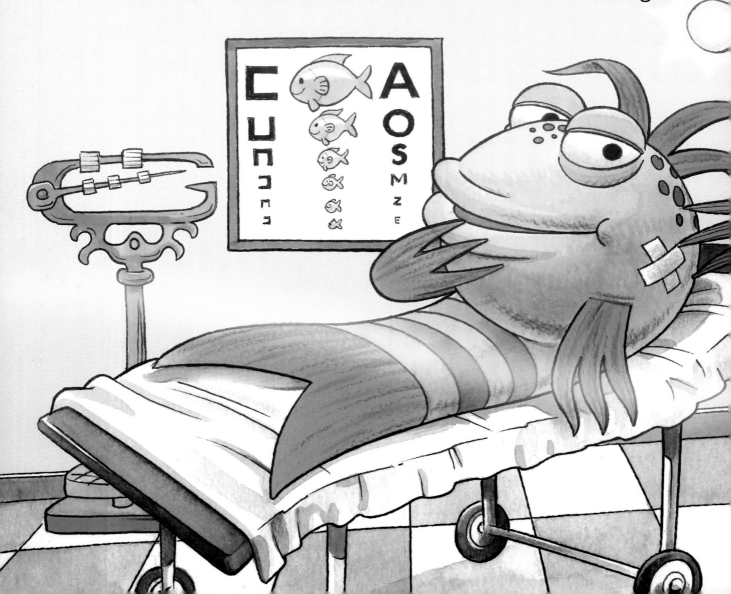

The doctor put them on, and then Mr. Fish was done!

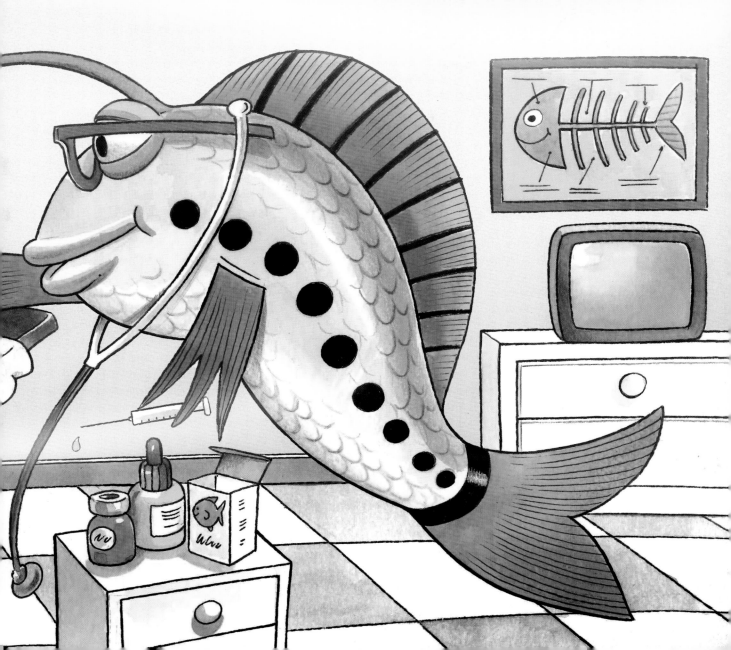

Mr. Eight was waiting for his friend. "How did it go?" he asked.
"Swimmingly well!" said Mr. Fish.

"A visit to the doctor is nothing to worry about," he assured a nervous-looking little fish whose turn was next. "My friend taught me that."

Mr. Fish's calm words helped her feel much better.

"You did a great job today," said the doctor to Mr. Fish.
"See you next time!"

"See you then!" said Mr. Fish, feeling healthy, happy, and strong.

I'M BRAVE

I'M BRAVE

SUPER STRONG

100% HEALTHY!

E

A

O

S